mary-kateandashley

TWO of a **kind**™

Diaries

D1152059

Look for these

titles:

Love-Set-Match

by Cathy Dubowski

from the series created by Robert Griffard
& Howard Adler

HarperCollins*Entertainment*
An Imprint of HarperCollins*Publishers*

A PARACHUTE PRESS BOOK

A PARACHUTE PRESS BOOK
Parachute Publishing, L.L.C.
156 Fifth Avenue
Suite 302
NEW YORK
NY 10010

First published in the USA by HarperEntertainment 2003
First published in Great Britain by HarperCollins*Entertainment* 2004
HarperCollins*Entertainment* is an imprint of HarperCollins*Publishers* Ltd,
77-85 Fulham Palace Road, Hammersmith, London W6 8JB

TWO OF A KIND characters, names and all related indicia are trademarks of
Warner Bros.™ & © 2000.
TWO OF A KIND books created and produced by
Parachute Publishing, L.C.C. in cooperation with Dualstar Publications,
a division of Dualstar Entertainment Group, Inc.

Cover photograph courtesy of Dualstar Entertainment Group, Inc. © 2003

The HarperCollins website address is
www.harpercollins.co.uk

1

ISBN 0 00 715885 8

Printed and bound in Great Britain by Clays Ltd, St Ives plc

Chapter 1

Sunday

Dear Diary,

Sorry if my handwriting is messy. I'm sitting on my duffel bag, waiting for the bus to arrive.

I can't believe I'm really going to camp in Michigan for the whole month! In the woods! With all the bugs and mud and shapeless T-shirts . . .

My sister, Mary-Kate, tried to cheer me up while we were in the parking lot, waiting for the Camp Evergreen bus to come. Dad dropped us at the bus terminal, unloaded our gear from the car, and drove off to find a parking spot.

"Stop moping, Ashley," Mary-Kate said. "We're going to sleep-away camp, not jail! It's supposed to be fun!"

"Sure," I said. "Fun for you. You like all that stuff. Sports and hiking and wild animals. But what about me? Do they have any activities I like at this camp? Shopping contests? Sunbathing hour? I checked the brochure, Mary-Kate, and I didn't see anything like that!"

I waved the Camp Evergreen brochure in her face. She snatched it away.

"Give me that," she said. We were surrounded by kids we didn't know, their parents, and lots of duffel bags. Mary-Kate was wearing her summer uniform of shorts and sneakers, her short blonde hair pulled back into a ponytail. I was the only girl in the parking lot wearing a sundress.

Dad is a professor. He has to go to Mexico for the summer to study some Aztec ruins. He didn't think we'd be happy in Chicago without him. Normally we'd go on a summer trip with our boarding school, White Oak Academy. But this year was different.

"Try to have fun for Dad's sake," Mary-Kate said. "He's so excited that we're going to his old camp."

Dad loves to tell stories about Camp Evergreen. He spent every summer there when he was a boy. He told us about the pranks he and his friends played, and the time his cabin won a pie-eating contest. He also hinted that there was a secret at Camp Evergreen – a secret we could find out only if we were campers there.

"Besides," Mary-Kate went on, "this is a chance to try new things! To do stuff you don't normally do."

I played with a strand of my blonde hair. My sister was right. "Okay," I agreed. "So what should I sign up for?"

Mary-Kate grinned. "Something you'd never do. Isn't it obvious?"

I frowned. I knew exactly what Mary-Kate was talking about. Sports. "All right, fine," I said. "But you have to try something new, too."

"What?" Mary-Kate asked. "Why?"

"Come on," I said. "I need moral support."

Mary-Kate sighed. "Okay. Like what?" she asked.

"I don't know," I said. "But definitely *no* sports."

Mary-Kate's eyes got wide. I knew she was starting to panic. She can't live without sports as much as I can't live without my strawberry shine lip gloss.

But she gave in. "Deal," she said.

We hooked pinkies on it. Then I took the brochure and skimmed the list of activities. There sure were a lot of sports at this camp. Which one would I choose?

Dad walked up just as the bus pulled into the parking lot. Mary-Kate and I hugged him.

"We'll miss you, Dad," I said.

"I'll miss you girls, too," Dad replied. His brown eyes were a little wet and he sniffled. "I can't believe it. My twelve-year-old daughters are off to Camp Evergreen! I hope you'll love it as much as I did."

"We will, Dad," Mary-Kate said.

Dad helped us load our duffel bags onto the bus. Then he kissed us goodbye and we climbed aboard.

I glanced at the brochure as I shuffled down the aisle towards an empty seat. They had tons of sports at Camp Evergreen, but none of them sounded good to me. Tetherball? Too tangly. Mountain climbing? They must be kidding! I'd get all sweaty, and then bugs would stick to the sweat. . . Ick.

 Suddenly – *oof!* I tripped over something in the aisle. I stumbled and almost fell into someone's lap! I caught my balance and looked down.

Two sky-blue eyes stared back at me. And they belonged to the cutest boy I have ever seen! Straight black hair, long eyelashes . . .

"Are you okay?" he asked me.

I didn't answer right away. I couldn't stop staring at those eyes. I hoped the lake at Camp Evergreen would be that blue.

"Hello?" the boy said. He waved his hand in front of my face. "Are you okay?"

"I'm fine," I replied. "Sorry – I'm so clumsy. . . "

"No, it's my fault," the boy said. "My bag was in the aisle."

He reached down to move his bag out of the way. I noticed something sticking out of it – a tennis racquet. Hmmm . . .

"Everyone, please take your seats!" the bus driver called.

Mary-Kate gave me a little push from behind. "Let's go, Ashley," she said.

The boy smiled at me. I smiled back. Then I hurried down the aisle and settled into a seat in the back. Mary-Kate sat beside me.

I peeked down the aisle to glance at the tennis player. Whoops! He caught me! He was staring back!

I leaned back in my seat and sighed. "Here," I said, handing the brochure back to Mary-Kate. "I don't need this any more."

"What do you mean?" she asked.

"I think I've found my sport," I told her.

Tennis, anyone?

Dear Diary,

I couldn't wait to get off the bus after that long ride. I looked around the campgrounds. "Isn't it beautiful?"

"Uh-huh," Ashley replied. She was staring at the boy with the tennis racquet. I don't think she was even talking about the camp.

But the camp *is* gorgeous! It's deep in the woods on a big, glassy lake called Lake Evergreen. The bus dropped us off at the Evergreen Lodge, the main building. The mess hall, the director's office, the nurse's office and a big meeting room are in the lodge. All the camp buildings are made of logs, and the lodge has a big front porch.

A tall girl with long dark hair said, "Welcome to Camp Evergreen! I'm Jill." She looked about seventeen. Ashley and I gave her our names and she checked us off on her clipboard. "You two are Tree Frogs," she told us. "That's the name of your cabin. And I'll be your counsellor!"

I glanced at Ashley, and she smiled. "She seems nice," Ashley whispered.

Jill told us to put our gear on a trolley and go inside for our camp welcome meeting. Ashley and I settled on the floor of the lodge with dozens of other kids, boys and girls aged six to twelve.

When everyone was settled, a stocky woman with short grey hair stood at the podium. "Welcome," she said. "I'm Nancy Grable, the director of Camp Evergreen."

Nancy told us that we'd each find an information packet with schedules, rules and activities on our

6

bunk beds. "Take today to look around and get a feel for the place," she said. "Tomorrow after breakfast everyone will sign up for any extra activities they want to do. Now go meet your cabin mates and have a wonderful time!"

The room buzzed as everybody stood up and headed towards their cabins.

"I wonder who our roommates will be," Ashley said.

We wandered down a path, past the little girls' cabins with a playground and swings, towards the lake. The boys all went to the south part of camp on the other side of the lodge.

I spotted a cabin with a green frog painted on the door. "This must be ours," I said. We pushed open the door.

Our cabin is small and cosy, with three bunks lined up against one wall and three on the other. There's one wardrobe and twelve drawers built into the wall – we each get two drawers. There's no bathroom – the girls' bathrooms are in a big bathhouse on the north side of the camp.

Only one girl was in the cabin when we got there. She had long, wavy dark hair and a flower painted on her cheek.

Ashley and I introduced ourselves.

"Hi, I'm Mindy," she said. "What's your sign?"

"Gemini," I said.

"Gemini! That's so cool," she said. "The symbol for Gemini is twins, and you're twins!" She started unpacking her duffel bag. She had lots of tie-dyed T-shirts and peasant blouses.

"I'm a Pisces," she told us.

A tall girl with glasses and short brown hair burst into the cabin. "Hello," she said, dropping her duffel on a bunk. "My name is Claire." She shook my hand, then Ashley's, then Mindy's, kind of stiffly. She carried a book under one arm. I glanced at the cover. *Understanding Physics*.

Wow, I thought. *What kind of girl reads a science textbook on summer vacation?*

"We'd better get this place organised," Claire said. She claimed her wardrobe space and her two drawers and got right to work unpacking.

"What's your sign, Claire?" Mindy asked.

Claire frowned. "I don't believe in that stuff."

"Let me guess," Mindy said. "Virgo, right? Virgos can be kind of uptight."

Claire clenched her jaw. "Hey – I'm not

uptight!"

I giggled. Claire was *so* uptight.

Claire relaxed a little. "Actually, my parents think I'm too serious. They sent me here last year to learn to loosen up and have some fun. But it didn't stick. So they're trying again this year."

Mindy threw an arm over Claire's shoulders. "Don't worry, Claire. We'll make sure you have fun this summer. Right, girls?"

"Right," Ashley said, but I wasn't so sure. I had a feeling Claire's idea of fun wasn't the same as Mindy's. Or mine.

Finally the last two girls arrived. Allison is small with curly blonde hair, and Emily has straight brown hair, freckles and a cute, chubby face.

"I'm kind of nervous," Emily admitted. "I've never been to sleep-away camp before."

"Claire and I will help you," Allison volunteered. "Claire was here last year, and this is my third year in a row. I've got four brothers and sisters at home. I begged my parents to let me come to camp. I had to get away!"

We all laughed. Mindy found out that Allison is a Taurus and Emily is a Cancer. Then she pulled a can out of her duffel bag and started spraying something around the room.

"Aromatherapy," Mindy explained. "'Summer

Mist.' It will help us all feel calm and serene."

"It smells like pine trees," I said.

"Ack!" Allison sneezed six times in a row. "Stop spraying that stuff! I think I'm allergic to it!"

"Oh, I'm so sorry!" Mindy put the can away.

"She's allergic to everything," Claire said.

"I am not!" Allison protested. "Just pollen, rag-weed, cats, dogs, dust, some trees, flowers, and a bunch of different plants."

I chose my two drawers and started putting my things away. Emily sat on her bunk, looking at some kind of big book. I walked across the room toward her and realised it was a scrapbook. There were mementos inside, along with pictures of her mom, her dad, her grandmother, her house, her room – even her bed! And about twenty pictures of her cat.

"What's your cat's name?" I asked her.

"Twinkles," she replied. "I sure miss him."

Diary, I get the feeling that Emily has never even spent the night at someone else's house. I made a mental note to be extra nice to her.

"That's a great scrapbook," I offered.

"Thanks," Emily said, smiling. "I make them all the time. One for every occasion."

Beep. Beep. Beep-beep.

What was that sound?

I turned towards a bunk at the back of the room. Claire had already unpacked. She sat on her bed, playing a handheld video game. She was so into it, she hardly noticed the rest of us. "Rats!" she cried out, staring at the screen. "I always miss that one!"

I sighed and went back to my unpacking. We were all so different. How would we ever get along for a whole month?

The screen door swung open and Jill walked in. "Hey there, campers. I wanted to let you know that there's a big 'Welcome Campers' cookout for dinner at five-thirty in the mess hall. With special guests."

"Special guests?" Allison said. "Who are they?"

Everyone looked up at Jill, and even Claire put down her computer game.

"Camp Ravenwood," Jill replied. "Evergreen's sister camp, just down the road from us."

"What's so special about them?" Claire asked.

"Well—" Jill paused. "It's a secret. A secret that is not allowed to leave the camp."

I glanced at Ashley. Could this be the secret Dad hinted about?

Chapter 2

Sunday

Dear Diary,

We had to beg, but finally Jill told us the secret of Camp Evergreen.

"A long time ago," Jill said, "Camp Evergreen and Camp Ravenwood were one big camp called Camp McArdle. It was started by two sisters named Martha and Ida McArdle. One day, Martha and Ida had a big fight."

"What about?" Ashley asked.

"No one knows for sure," Jill said. "But whatever the reason, they split their camp in two and named them Evergreen and Ravenwood. And they never spoke to each other again."

"Wow!" I said.

"Even after they split up, Martha and Ida kept competing with each other. Everything Evergreen did, Ravenwood tried to do better. Who had the best tennis team? Who had the fastest canoe? They organised all kinds of races and competitions, games that continue even to this day!"

"Excellent!" Ashley said. My sister isn't wild about sports, but she definitely loves competition!

"Each contest is worth one point," Jill told us. "There's a board in the lodge where we keep track of the score. Whichever camp has the most points at the end of the summer wins the camp competition!"

"Who won last year?" Claire asked.

Jill frowned. "Ravenwood creamed us. They won the competitions *and* the Underground Challenge."

"The Underground Challenge?" I asked. "What's that?"

Jill moved in a little closer. "That's the secret part. Everyone knows about the regular games. But only the counsellors and the older campers know about the Underground Challenge."

"Tell us about it!" Claire insisted.

"Before their big fight, Martha and Ida had their portrait painted together," Jill went on. "When they stopped speaking, Martha, who started Evergreen, kept the portrait. But then the campers from Ravenwood stole it! The next year Evergreen campers stole it ."

"Who has it now?" I asked.

"Ravenwood," Jill said. "They've had it three years in a row! We have to get it back. If we can steal the portrait and keep it until the end of the summer, we'll be the *real* winners."

Wow. A secret competition! How cool was that?

"We are so going to steal it," Claire said.

"Totally," Ashley added.

"That's the spirit!" Jill cheered. "I was hoping my

cabin would be smart enough, brave enough and crafty enough to steal the portrait this year."

"You can count on us," I said. "Right, girls?"

"Right!" the others said. I thought Emily looked a little scared, though.

I couldn't wait for five-thirty to come. I wanted to size up our Ravenwood competition. Jill showed us around the camp, and then we all took a quick dip in the lake.

Finally it was time to go to the picnic field for the cookout. All the campers from Ravenwood came. There must have been at least a hundred kids there. Lines were already forming at the two big barbecues.

"Let's grab some food before the lines get too long," Claire said. We all picked up plates and got in line. Two boys joined the line behind us. They looked about our age. One of them was skinny with bushy, curly black hair. He needed a haircut, and he was wearing knee socks, which looked kind of goofy. The other one was really cute, athletic-looking with light brown hair and dark brown eyes.

"Hey, girls," the bushy-haired one said. "Are you Ravenwood or Evergreen?" He was talking to all of us, but he was looking right at Mindy.

"Evergreen," Mindy replied. "We're Tree Frogs."

"You'd better be from Evergreen, too," Claire said, "or we won't talk to you."

"Don't worry, we are," the boy said. "I'm Jason, and this is Patrick." He pointed to the cute boy with the brown eyes. "We're in Rattlesnake."

Jason kept staring at Mindy the whole time we were talking. I think he likes her!

Mindy turned to Jason and Patrick. "What sign are you?" she asked Patrick.

Patrick looked confused. "Me? Uh, I don't know."

"I'm a Scorpio," Jason said.

"Really?" Mindy said. "Scorpios get along really well with Pisces."

Ashley and I giggled.

Patrick turned to me. "Do you know what she's talking about?" he asked.

"Astrology," I told him. "She's totally into it."

"Can she tell fortunes?" Patrick asked. "Because I'd like to know who's going to win the Camp Games this year."

"I can tell you that without using astrology," I said. "Evergreen's going to win."

"How do you know?" Patrick asked.

"Because I'm going to make sure that we do," I said.

He looked impressed. "All right, a girl who takes charge. I like that."

Two of a Kind Diaries

I felt my face start to get red. Was Patrick flirting with me?

We finally reached the barbecue table. We loaded our plates with hamburgers, hot dogs, chicken and potato salad. Then we wandered through the huge crowd, trying to find an empty table.

"There are some seats." Allison pointed out a long picnic table. Four kids – two girls and two boys – were sitting at one end, but there was enough room for the rest of us.

"Are these seats taken?" Ashley asked.

"Only if you're from Evergreen," one of the boys answered.

The other boy snickered and said, "Good one, Pete. Ravenwood rules!"

Claire put her plate down. "We *are* from Evergreen," she said, "but we're sitting here anyway."

I want to beat Ravenwood in the games. But I don't see any reason to be mean to them, so I introduced everybody.

"This is Pete, Rob and Lindsay," a red-haired girl said. "And I'm Shawna."

"Remember our names," Pete warned. "You'll be seeing a lot of us at the games."

"Yeah, the backs of our heads," Lindsay added. "When we pass you in every race."

"No way," Patrick said. "Evergreen's going to take it all this year."

"And we mean *everything*," Claire said. "Including the ultimate prize."

Everybody knew what she was talking about. The portrait.

Rob laughed. "We've had the portrait for three years in a row. Evergreen will never get it back."

"All this competition stuff is kind of silly, don't you think?" Emily said.

"Only a loser wouldn't be into it," Rob replied.

Emily shrank back. She looked like she was going to cry.

I'd heard enough. I tried to like these Ravenwood kids, but picking on Emily was too mean!

"Only a loser would be a jerk to someone they don't even know," I told Rob.

Ashley and our new friends all cheered. Then I turned to the other Ravenwood kids. "Oh, and about that portrait? The kids in the Eagle bunk stole it" – I glanced at my watch – "about fifteen minutes ago."

Okay, so that wasn't true, but I had to say something!

"No way!" Rob shouted. The Ravenwood

campers jumped up from the table and ran off.

"Who stole the portrait?" Emily asked.

"No one – yet. But Evergreen *will* get it," I vowed. Then Ashley shot me a look. I knew exactly what she was thinking.

How were we going to do that?

Dear Diary,

After breakfast this morning we were given schedules for our required activities – swimming, nature walks, stuff like that. Then we got to sign up for other things. I went straight for the tennis sign-up sheet.

I was hoping I'd get to wear one of those cute little tennis dresses, but no. The tennis team, girls and boys, all wear the same thing – white shorts and white Camp Evergreen T-shirts. Still, as long as that cute guy with the blue eyes was on the tennis team, it would be worth it.

Allison signed up for tennis, too. I was so glad – at least I'd know someone at practice.

Practice started at nine-thirty, right after the Tree Frogs' morning swim. Allison and I grabbed our racquets and headed for the courts. About twenty-five kids, boys and girls, gathered in the bleachers. I scanned the crowd for the boy

18

on the bus. He wasn't there. Then I spotted him out on the court, volleying with a man in tennis whites. I figured the man had to be the coach.

Thwack! The cute guy smacked the ball hard. The coach scrambled across the court to hit it back. *Thwack!* The boy came right back at him.

"That guy is almost as good as the coach," Allison whispered to me.

The coach stopped playing and came over to the bleachers to talk to us.

"Wow, we have a big turnout this year," the coach said. "I'm Coach Worth. This is my son, Andrew." The boy came around from the other side of the net, guzzling a bottle of water.

No wonder Andrew is such a good player, I thought. *His dad is a tennis coach!*

Andrew spotted me in the bleachers and grinned. I almost melted. He's so cute!

"Tennis is not just a game," Coach Worth said. "It's a serious sport. I expect a lot of hard work from everyone on my team. We have a big match against Ravenwood in a couple of weeks. Their team is very strong. But this year I'm determined to beat them!"

"This guy is really serious," Allison whispered to me.

"Yeah," I agreed. "This is summer camp. We're just here to have a good time."

Coach Worth paused, silently counting the crowd of kids. "I'm afraid I can't use all of you," he announced. "There's room for only sixteen people on the team. So I'll be holding tryouts, starting in five minutes."

My stomach filled with butterflies. "Tryouts?" I gasped. I wasn't expecting that. "What if I don't make the team?"

The boy next to me said, "Don't worry, you have a good chance of making it. Coach has to cut only nine people."

I sighed, thinking back to the tennis lessons I took when I was little. The result wasn't pretty. "You haven't seen me play," I said.

"Line up on the court, everyone," Coach Worth called. "You'll each take a turn volleying with Andrew, one at a time. Let's take the girls first."

"Oh, no!" I groaned. "We have to play against Andrew? He's so good!"

"Don't worry," the boy next to me said. "He won't try to show you up. He's a nice guy."

"How do you know?" Allison asked.

"He's my best friend," the guy said. I looked at him a little more closely. He was nice-looking, with short, spiky brown hair and an easy smile. But he wasn't nearly as cute as Andrew.

Love-Set-Match

"I'm Ashley," I said. "And this is Allison."

"Ashley and Allison," the guy said. "Double A. I'm Max. You'd better get in line, Double A, or you'll miss your turns."

Allison and I hurried down to the court and got in line. When it was my turn to volley, my hands were sweatier than ever. I was nervous about making the team – and totally distracted every time I looked at Andrew. How could I keep my eye on the ball when *he* was across the net from me?

He lobbed an easy shot to me. I got into position, swiped my racquet, and missed. Nothing but air.

"Don't worry," Andrew called. "Try again."

He tapped the ball gently over the net. *Eye on the ball, eye on the ball,* I told myself. This time I hit it, but it plopped into the net.

At least I was improving.

"You'll get it this time," Andrew said. He served, and the ball seemed to come right to my racquet. I smacked it over the net.

"Woo-hoo!" Andrew shouted. He did a fancy spin and hit the ball back to me between his legs. I was laughing so hard, I missed the next shot.

"Andrew – quit fooling around," Coach Worth warned. "And Miss—" He was talking to me!

"Ashley Burke," I told him.

"You'd better start concentrating if you want to make this team," he scolded.

"Yes, sir," I said. I prepared myself for the next shot. *Concentrate, concentrate.* Andrew winked at me. Then he served the ball. I hit it back, and we volleyed for a few minutes. I actually got the ball over the net four times in a row!

My last shot went out-of-bounds.

"That's enough," Coach Worth called. "Next."

Allison was next. Andrew jogged to the net and waved me over. "You did great," he said. "Will you be my hitting partner during practice?"

My heart thumped. He wanted me to be his hitting partner! He must like me. It couldn't be the way I play tennis.

"Sure," I said.

"Andrew!" Coach Worth yelled. "The next girl is waiting!"

I hurried off the court. If I was Andrew's hitting partner, I'd get to hang with him every day!

But it wouldn't happen if I didn't make the team. And somehow I got the feeling Coach Worth didn't like me too much.

Diary, I can hardly wait until tomorrow to find out. Will I make it?

Monday

Dear Diary,

"Don't worry, Ashley," I said. "Maybe you're not Wimbledon material, but I bet you'll make the team."

"I hope so." She sighed and pushed her tray away. We'd just finished lunch in the mess hall. The food isn't too bad here – lots of fruit, all kinds of sandwiches, and freshly baked cookies for dessert!

"What about you?" Ashley asked. "What activity did you sign up for?"

I'd been dreading this moment, Diary. When I read the list of activities, I saw one I really wanted to do. And I signed up for it. But Ashley wasn't going to like it.

"Wilderness Challenge," I admitted. "It's one of the biggest races in the Camp Games!"

"Wilderness Challenge!" Ashley cried. "But that's not something new. You love that sort of stuff. And it sounds like a sport to me. What about our deal?"

"It's not really a sport," I said, hoping she'd buy it. "It's more like becoming one with nature!" Even though we

One with Nature

23

spent the whole morning hiking, running and climbing over obstacles. "And anyway, I thought of another thing I can do that is totally not a sport at all."

"What?" Ashley looked suspicious.

"It's called Big Sisters/Little Sisters," I said. "They pair an older camper with a six- or seven-year-old. I don't have much baby-sitting experience, but I have lots of experience being a sister. And how hard could it be to hang out with a seven-year-old a few afternoons a week?"

I acted very confident about the whole thing. But actually I was nervous about it. What was I supposed to do with a little kid?

The first meeting was that afternoon in the lodge. There were twenty older girls and twenty little girls. Nancy Grable, the camp director, ran the meeting.

"I'm glad we have such a good turnout for the Big Sister programme this summer," Nancy said. "Having a Big or Little Sister makes camp feel more like family."

Well, I already have a sister at the camp, but what's one more?

While Nancy talked, I looked at the little girls sitting across the room. Which one would be my Little Sister?

The little girls sat in groups, whispering and giggling.

But one girl sat apart from the rest, by herself.

Poor kid, I thought. She had short, messy blonde hair and a cute little upturned nose. The knees on her jeans were scuffed and dirty, just like mine always were when I was her age.

Maybe she's a tomboy like I was, I thought. *Is that why she's not sitting with the other girls?*

Finally Nancy said, "So, Big Sisters, you can expect to spend three activity periods a week with your Little Sister – just an hour each time. If you want to spend more time together, that's up to you." Then Nancy assigned the Big Sisters to their little sisters. And guess what? Nancy paired me up with the tomboy! Her name is Jessie.

"Now go meet each other," Nancy said. "We have a craft activity you can do to help you get to know your new Sister better. Have fun!"

Everyone stood up and milled around. I moved toward the scruffy little girl. She sat in the corner, kicking the leg of a chair.

"Hi, Jessie," I said. "I'm Mary-Kate. How do you like camp so far?"

Jessie shrugged. "It's okay."

"Do you have any sisters at home?" I asked.

"Nope," she answered. "But I have two big

brothers. Jack is ten and Ben is almost thirteen!"

"I don't have any brothers," I told her. "But I'm looking forward to being your Big Sister."

She gazed up at me with eyes like big, shiny black buttons. "Really?"

"Sure!" I said. "What kinds of things do you like to do? Do you like to play with dolls?"

"No," she said. "I like to play trucks with my brothers. And we play soccer in the backyard a lot. And I like to shoot baskets in the driveway."

"Just like me!" I said. "I love sports, too."

"All right, everyone!" Nancy clapped her hands. "If you've found your new Sister, come over to the craft tables. You can all make necklaces to give to your Big or Little Sister."

I took Jessie's hand and led her to the craft table. We sat down near a bunch of other girls and got to work. There were boxes of dry macaroni, spools of string, and paints and brushes.

Jessie grabbed two pieces of macaroni and stuck them in her nose. "How do I look?" she asked.

Some of the other little girls were making grossed-out faces at Jessie. I thought Jessie looked kind of funny.

She took the macaroni out of her nose and watched what I was doing. "I think I'll paint my macaroni beads first," I said. "Then I'll string them together in a pattern."

I grabbed a pot of red paint and a pot of blue paint and a paintbrush. I carefully painted some macaroni bits red and blue. Jessie watched me and copied everything I did.

"You don't have to do yours exactly like mine," I told her. "You can use different colours."

"I like the way you're doing it," Jessie said.

When the paint was dry, I strung my necklace together. "I think this would look better with a few white pieces," I said. "Like a flag. Red, white and blue."

"Me, too," Jessie agreed.

I painted some macaronis white, and again Jessie copied me. When we were finished, I tied a knot in each string.

"Mary-Kate," Jessie said, holding out her necklace. "This is for you."

I bent down my head and she hung the necklace around my neck. "Thank you, Jessie. It's beautiful. And this is for you." I put my necklace on her. She fingered the necklace as if it were made of diamonds.

"Now we both have the same necklace," she said. "Everyone will know that we're camp Sisters!"

I was so glad I'd decided to be a Big Sister. Jessie

was so sweet. And it felt good to have someone look up to me so much.

When the meeting broke up, I offered to walk Jessie back to her cabin. I noticed that all the other little girls walked together in groups. But no one asked Jessie to join their group.

"Don't you want to go play with your friends?" I asked her.

Jessie shook her head. "No. I like you better."

I took her hand and we walked to her cabin. She was staring at my green polo shirt and white shorts. "Your clothes are nice. Did you make that hair clip?" she asked me.

I pulled the sparkly pink clip from my hair and stared at it. I'd forgotten I was wearing it.

"Are you kidding?" I said. "I can't make stuff like this." I handed it to her and she stared at it as if it were made of solid gold.

"You can keep it," I told her.

"Really?" she cried. She grabbed a handful of spiky hair and shoved the clip over it. The hair stood straight up. I tried not to laugh.

"Thank you so much, Mary-Kate!" she said. "It's the best gift I ever got!"

She threw her arms around my waist and hugged me. "I'm so glad you're my Big Sister," she said. "Now I can hang out with you all the time!"

"I'm glad, too, Jessie," I said, hugging her back.

I couldn't understand why the other little girls didn't want to play with Jessie. She was great!

Dear Diary,

The Tree Frogs went on their first nature walk this afternoon. Allison and I walked together. It was sort of fun, but every time Debbie, the nature counsellor, picked a fern to show us, Allison started sneezing. And I walked right into a spider's web! Yuck!

Finally it was four o'clock. I'd been waiting all day for four o'clock to come. That's when Coach Worth said he'd post the tennis team list.

We stopped at our cabin so Allison could get her nose drops. Then I dragged her to the tennis courts.

"I can't look," I said as we stood in front of the notice board where the list was posted. I covered my eyes with my hands while Allison checked the board.

"Wow," she said.

"Wow?" I asked. "Is that a good wow or a bad wow?"

"Good wow!" Allison squealed. "We both made the team!"

I opened my eyes and scanned the list. There it was! My name!

I couldn't believe it. I actually tried out for a sport and made the team! Mary-Kate would be so proud of me!

I grabbed Allison's hand. "I'm so excited! Let's go get our racquets and practise!"

We had an hour and a half before we had to be in the mess hall for dinner. So we ran to the cabin, grabbed our racquets and hurried back to the tennis courts. Allison and I volleyed for a while. I didn't realise what a good player she is. She's on her school team at home. And she told me that I was getting better very quickly. And I think I actually got better since yesterday!

It was almost dinnertime, so we quit and started back to our cabin. The whole camp is very woodsy. Sometimes on the trails between cabins you feel like you're in the middle of a forest. The trails wind and twist, and you can't see anything but trees.

Allison was saying, "You know that chalk they use to line the tennis courts? I think I'm allergic—"

She stopped talking because we heard a loud voice in the woods. A man's voice. It came from somewhere ahead of us on the path.

"Son, you're twelve now," the man said. "It's time to get serious."

"That's Coach Worth," I whispered to Allison. "He must be talking to Andrew."

We stood frozen in the path as the voices slowly moved closer and closer to us.

"You've got a lot of talent, Andrew, but that isn't enough. You won't get anywhere without hard work and discipline. So this summer I want you to focus on tennis and only tennis."

"But, Dad—" Andrew protested.

"No buts," Coach Worth insisted. "You'll thank me for this later – when you're a top tennis player."

They kept walking towards us. Their voices got louder as they came closer.

"They'll see us soon," Allison whispered. "Let's hide!" She grabbed my hand and pulled me behind a big rock on the side of the path.

Soon Andrew and his dad came into view and walked past us.

"Dad, it's summer," Andrew said. "I promise to practise hard. But I want to have some fun, too!"

"Listen, son," Coach Worth said, "I know what's best for you. So for the rest of the summer it's all tennis all the time. No other sports, no late nights, and most of all, no girls. They're very distracting. . . "

They wandered down the path and out of sight. I couldn't hear what they were saying anymore.

My heart sank as Coach Worth's words echoed in my ears.

No girls? But . . . what about me?

Chapter 4

Tuesday

Dear Diary,

Does Andrew like me? I'm not sure. But what difference does it make? Even if Andrew *does* like me, he's not allowed to hang around with any girls!

One thing's for sure – *I* like *him!* But I can't let Coach Worth see that. He could kick me off the team!

So when I saw Andrew at breakfast this morning I just said hi, then sat with the other Tree Frogs. Then at tennis practice I tried to play it cool and stay away from Andrew.

The coach had set up a practice match between me and Allison. We were volleying when Andrew came over to give us some pointers. "Your grip is off, Ashley," he said. He stood behind me and adjusted my hand on my racquet.

"How's that?" he asked me. "Better?"

"Uh-huh," I said. I could hardly talk. Being close to Andrew made me nervous. I glanced over towards the coach. He was staring right at us!

And he wasn't the only one. Every girl on the tennis team was watching me and Andrew.

I couldn't blame them. Andrew is so cute. Who wouldn't want extra attention from him?

"Now try your serve again," Andrew said.

I served, and it was much better. "See," Andrew said. "It really helps."

"I think I need some water," Allison said. She smiled at me, and I could tell she figured that something was going on. "I'll be back in a few minutes."

"Let's play until Allison comes back." Andrew trotted to the other side of the court. "Serve it. Let's see what you've got."

I tossed the ball in the air and smacked it as hard as I could. Unfortunately, that's not very hard. The  ball floated through the air and bounced on the court right in front of Andrew's racquet. Easy shot for him. But at least my serve was in.

Andrew whiffed his racquet through the air, missing the ball, and spun around three times. "What a shot!" he yelled. "You aced me!"

I laughed. Then he served to me, not too hard, and I watched how he did it. I hit the ball back, and we volleyed until I smacked one into the net. My turn to serve again. This time my serve was a little better. But it was still an easy shot for Andrew.

"Bzzzzzz!" He waved his racquet like a fly swatter and slapped at the ball as if it were a mosquito. "Got it!" he shouted, smacking the ball to the ground.

I laughed again. But Coach Worth glared at us from the sidelines. *Better get serious*, I thought.

"Let's take a break," I called. "I'm thirsty."

We headed for the water cooler. Allison was still there, sipping her water *really* slowly. Andrew reached for a cup before I had a chance to and poured me some water. His hand brushed mine as he gave me the cup. My hand tingled. I smiled and stared at my tennis shoes. All of a sudden I felt shy.

"Listen," he said. "I'd better go practise with my dad. But do you want to meet me down at the lake after dinner tonight?"

"Sure," I said. *Stay cool, stay cool*, I told myself. But inside I was so excited. I was going to hang out alone with Andrew!

Dear Diary,

Today was the first competition between Evergreen and Ravenwood – a huge tug-of-war held at Ravenwood. The tug-of-war was divided by age groups. Ashley and I hadn't signed up, but the whole camp was going to Ravenwood to watch. Maybe we'd have a chance to scope out the place, too!

"Excellent," Patrick said to me in the mess hall at

lunchtime today. He and Jason were sitting with me, Ashley and our cabin mates. "This is our chance to check out the enemy camp. Once we find out where the portrait is, we can make a plan to steal it."

So after lunch the counsellors trooped us all down to Ravenwood. I couldn't help noticing that Jason kind of stuck to Mindy, even though his bunk was supposed to be behind us. And Patrick walked beside me the whole way, too. Does he like me? It's hard to tell. But maybe.

Since this was the first competition of the summer, there was a ceremony. Ravenwood's director welcomed everybody. Then he shook hands with our director, Nancy, and she made a speech about sportsmanship. About a hundred kids sat in an open field, waiting for the tug-of-war to start. And I had a feeling most of the older Evergreen campers were on the lookout for the portrait, just like us.

"The true spirit of sportsmanship is not winning or losing," Nancy said into her microphone, "but friendship and understanding."

"Let's skip the speech," Claire whispered. "Now's our chance to look for that portrait."

I glanced toward our counsellor, Jill. She was talking with some other counsellors near the podium where Nancy was making her speech.

The field was crowded with kids. No one would

miss us if we slipped
away for a few minutes.

I passed the message to
Ashley, who passed it to
Allison, who passed it to Emily, who passed it to Mindy,
who passed it to Jason, who passed it to Patrick.

We were off to find the portrait. First stop,
Ravenwood's main lodge.

"What if someone catches us?" Emily asked nervously.

"We'll just say we were looking for the bathroom," I told her.

The Ravenwood camp had the same layout as
Evergreen, so it was pretty easy to find our way
around. We sneaked into the lodge. "It's not here,"
Patrick said, glancing around.

Next we crept into the main entrance hall. There
it was. Hanging over the big stone fireplace was an
old painting of two plain-looking women.

"They left it right out in the open," Allison said.
"No one's even guarding it!"

"Let's just grab it and run," Patrick suggested.

"We'll never make it back to Evergreen," I pointed
out. "We can't get back without passing the playing
field. Someone will see us for sure."

"Maybe we could cover it with something,"
Mindy suggested.

"Whatever we do, let's hurry," Jason said. "Before—"

"Hey!" someone shouted. "What are you doing in here?"

We all froze. Busted! The Ravenwood kids caught us!

I slowly turned around. In the doorway stood a little girl.

I relaxed. "Jessie! What are you doing here?"

"Looking for you!" Jessie said. "I saw you guys sneak away, so I followed you."

She was wearing a green T-shirt and white shorts – kind of like what I wore yesterday. And the pink clip I gave her was perched on her head.

That's so cute, I thought. *She wants to be like me!*

"Who's that?" Jason asked.

"This is my Little Sister, Jessie," I explained. "It's all right – she's on our side."

"What are you guys doing here?" Jessie asked.

I paused. The Underground Challenge was a secret for older campers only. I wasn't sure it was a good idea to let Jessie in on it.

But Emily blurted out, "We're trying to steal this picture. It's a camp competition."

Jessie's eyes got big. "Wow. Can I help you?"

"No," I said, frowning at Emily. "This is only for big kids."

From the field we heard the blast of a whistle. "The tug-of-war is starting!" Claire cried. "Let's go!"

We hurried back to the field – just in time to see one of the Evergreen teams tumble to the ground. Then another. And another! When it was all over, we had lost.

The game broke up. The Evergreen teams dusted the dirt from their shorts. Pete and Shawna walked by us, laughing.

"That was almost too easy!" Pete said. Then he spotted us. "Look who it is," he said. "The Evergreen losers. How does it feel?"

I glanced at Patrick. He clenched his fists. I was mad, too.

"Who cares if you won this round," I said. "Don't get used to it."

"Yeah," Claire said. "We're going to win the rest."

Pete and Shawna laughed and walked away. "They're so lame," Shawna said to Pete. "It's sad."

"Lame?" Claire echoed.

"Sad?" Ashley repeated.

"They did *not* just say that," Jason chimed in.

Diary, there's no way we can lose the competition now. The honor of Evergreen is at stake!

Chapter 5

Tuesday

Dear Diary,

"I can hardly eat," Claire complained. "And I usually love spaghetti."

My whole cabin, plus Jason and Patrick, were sitting together at dinner.

"Come on, Claire," Ashley said. "We'll get them next time."

Eric, the counsellor in charge of the Wilderness Challenge, stopped by our table. "Hey, Mary-Kate," he said. "Tough loss today, huh?"

"Yeah," I said. "But we'll beat them in the Wilderness Challenge."

"That's why I'm here," Eric said. "We need one more person for our Wilderness Challenge team. Know anybody who wants to do it?"

"I'll do it," Patrick quickly volunteered.

"Great," Eric said. "We'll meet at the practice course in the woods tomorrow morning right after breakfast. Eight-thirty sharp. I'll see both of you there."

I glanced at Patrick out of the corner of my eye. What made him volunteer? Is it camp spirit? Or does he want to spend a little more time around me?

Both, I hope.

Two of a Kind Diaries

Dear Diary,

Wow! What a night!

It started after dinner. I went down to the lake to meet Andrew. He was waiting for me on the dock. The sun was setting behind the trees on the other side of the lake.

I sat beside him. "Hey," he said, smiling at me. "Can you believe we lost the tug-of-war today? That's the one event Evergreen always wins."

"Really?" I said. "Do you think we're in trouble?"

"Well, Ravenwood is usually good at all the water sports," Andrew said. "Swimming, canoeing – all that stuff. Though last year Brooke and I won our leg of the sailing race. Nobody could beat us."

Brooke? "Who's Brooke?" I asked.

"She's one of my best friends," Andrew explained. "She and Max and I were like the Three Musketeers last summer. She's coming to camp late. Her parents took her to Europe first. She's really cool. You'll like her."

Hmmm. Maybe I will like Brooke. But I didn't like the sound of this. I ploughed ahead.

"Anyway, I'm sure we'll beat Ravenwood at tennis this year with you on our team," I said.

"I guess." He sighed. "The problem is, I'm not sure I even want to be on the team."

"What?" I gasped. "But you're so good! I think it

must feel great to be that amazingly good at a sport."

"But you're pretty good," Andrew told her. "I can tell you don't practise that much. But if you did, you'd be a great player."

I slipped off my sandals and kicked my feet in the water. Did he really mean that? I guess it doesn't matter. There's no way I'll ever practise a sport as much as he does.

"Why would you want to quit?" I asked.

"I guess I don't," he admitted. "I love playing. It's just my dad – he's so intense about it. He wants me to turn pro. He's always pushing me about 'my career.' But who wants a career? I'm twelve!"

I didn't know what to say to that. It was a big problem, but I was glad that Andrew trusted me enough to talk about it. We watched as the sun set and a few bright stars came out. Andrew told me some funny stories about camp last summer, but I couldn't get his problem out of my head.

"You're too talented to give up tennis," I told him. "But maybe you should talk to your dad. Tell him how you feel. He might understand."

"Maybe I will," Andrew decided. "Thanks."

He leaned close and kissed me on the cheek.

I grinned. Andrew was great!

Andrew checked his glow-in-the dark watch. "We'd better go," he said. "It's almost time for lights-out."

We didn't say anything as we walked back towards the cabins. Once in a while the back of his hand brushed against mine. We stopped where the path forked. To the left were the girls' cabins, to the right, the boys'.

"Well, see you on the courts tomorrow morning," Andrew said. "Thanks for meeting me, Ashley. I like talking to you."

"I like talking to you, too," I said. "Bye!"

I flew down the path to Tree Frogs. I couldn't wait to tell Mary-Kate what happened!

I burst into the cabin. Everyone was gathered around Claire's bunk. They looked upset.

"What's the matter?" I asked.

"Ashley, look at this!" Mary-Kate cried. She held up a piece of paper. "We found this tacked to our cabin door!"

I grabbed the paper and read it.

WARNING!
To the losers at Evergreen:
Ravenwood is going to make camp history this year. We're going to win every event in the competition! And you'll never get your hands on the portrait! So give it up and go play on the swings!
Your sworn enemies,
The Ravenwood Winners

There were no names on the note, but I knew who wrote it: Pete, Shawna, Lindsay and Rob.

"What are they trying to prove with this?" I held up the note. "That they're jerks?"

"We already *know* that," Mary-Kate said.

"That whole camp must be full of Aries," Mindy said.

"Mindy, what are you talking about?" Claire asked.

"Aries is a very warlike sign," Mindy explained.

Claire rolled her eyes.

"No more playing around," Emily said firmly.

Everybody stared at her.

"I thought you didn't like this competitive stuff," Allison said.

Emily shrugged. "These Ravenwood kids are really starting to bug me."

"You're right," I said. "We've got to teach them a lesson."

"We sure do," Claire said. "So listen up, everybody. Mindy and I have come up with a foolproof plan to steal that portrait!"

Oops! Time for lights-out. I'll tell you Claire's awesome plan tomorrow!

Chapter 6

Wednesday

Dear Diary,

I was really looking forward to Wilderness Challenge practice today. And when Patrick volunteered to join yesterday, I got even more excited about it!

It's a great way to get to know him better. Plus I'm pretty good at outdoor sports, so I thought I might impress him.

Diary, I was so wrong! What a disaster!

It started out okay. Eric led us to the practice course in the woods and told us what we'd be doing. First we had to climb a tree, then cross a narrow rope bridge. Then we had to slide down a rope and climb the "spider's web," which is a big net made of ropes. Next we were supposed to swing like Tarzan over a creek and run down a muddy trail back to the beginning of the course.

"Pretty tough, huh?" Patrick said to me. He didn't look too worried, though.

"Yeah," I agreed. "Get ready for rope burn." But secretly I thought, *I'm going to ace this thing.*

"Let's do a practice run," Eric said. "I'll time each of you. Patrick, you start. Go!"

Patrick scrambled up the tree like a cat. He ran easily across the rope bridge. *He's a really good ath-*

lete, I thought. Now I *really* wanted to make a good impression on him.

Eric blew his whistle. "Mary-Kate, go!"

I climbed the tree so fast, I surprised myself. Then I raced across the wobbly rope bridge, no problem. I slid down the rope to the ground and ran to the spider's web. Patrick was just getting off the spider's web. I was catching up to him!

After swinging over the creek I was hard on Patrick's heels. We ran down the muddy trail, and I passed him. That's when disaster struck.

I was running fast, trying not to slip in the mud. All of a sudden – "Hey! Mary-Kate!"

Jessie popped out from behind a tree and stood right in front of me, waving her arms.

"Jessie, look out!" I cried. I swerved so I wouldn't knock her down – and lost my balance.

Splat! I fell face first in the mud!

Patrick was right be-
hind me. He didn't have
any time to stop, so he
jumped around me.

Jessie hurried over.
"Mary-Kate, are you all right? Why did you fall?"

I sat up and wiped the mud from my eyes. "Jessie, what are you doing here?" I asked. "I'm in the middle of a practice race!"

"I was looking for you," Jessie said. "I'm supposed to be at swimming, but I wanted to see you so I went to the lodge and looked up your schedule."

I had to admit, if I wasn't so embarrassed I might have thought it was cute.

"Jessie!" a girl called. She appeared in an opening in the bushes. She stopped when she saw us. "There you are," she said, out of breath. "Didn't we have a talk about this?"

"Sorry, Lisa," Jessie said. I assumed Lisa was her counsellor.

Lisa took Jessie's hand. "Come on, Jess. Before we both get in trouble." And then they were gone.

Patrick jogged over to me. I could tell he was trying not to laugh as I sat in the mud. "Are you okay?" he asked.

"Fine," I muttered, wiping some dirt off my cheek. Does it get any more embarrassing than that?

Dear Diary,

All the way to the tennis courts this morning, Allison and I talked about our secret portrait-stealing plan.

"We need to strike as soon as possible," I told Allison. "I heard the Iguanas and the Hawks are plotting to steal the portrait, too. It will be great if they get it – but I want Tree Frogs to be the heroes!"

Love-Set-Match

"Me, too," Allison agreed. "I'm just worried that the plan is a little complicated."

The plan *is* complicated. Mindy looked at her astrological charts after lights-out last night and said the perfect time to put it into action was when the moon and the North Star are aligned. That brings the most success.

I had no idea what Mindy was talking about, but whatever. We can use all the luck we can get.

When we got to the courts, Andrew was volleying with Coach Worth. The coach slammed a shot to the corner of Andrew's court. Andrew missed it.

"Hustle, hustle!" Coach Worth yelled at him. "What's wrong with you today, Andrew?"

"Nothing," Andrew said.

"Well, you look tired," the coach said. "I hope you're getting enough sleep."

"Don't worry, Dad, I am," Andrew said.

"Then let's see some energy!" Coach barked.

Uh-oh, I thought. Coach Worth seemed to be in a bad mood. He'd told Andrew "no girls," but last night Andrew met me at the lake. . . And now Coach was pretty cranky with him. Did the coach find out about it?

"Let's warm up over there," I said to Allison, pointing out the court farthest away from Andrew and his dad.

47

Allison and I volleyed hard. The big match against Ravenwood is coming up soon! And I really want to beat them.

The rest of the team arrived and started practising. Andrew's friend Max stopped at our court. "Hey, it's Double A," he said. "Ashley, I've got something for you."

"For me?" I walked over to him, and he handed me a sealed envelope. "What is this?"

Max shrugged. "I'm just the mailman. But it's from Andrew. He stayed up really late last night writing about twenty-seven versions of it."

"Max! Are you still on the team?" Coach Worth shouted.

"Gotta go," Max said. He hurried to his court.

I couldn't believe it – a letter from Andrew! I tore open the envelope. Here's what it said:

Dear Ashley,

I'm so glad we met by the lake last night. The first time I saw you, when you tripped over my bag on the bus, I thought you were the prettiest girl I've ever seen. But now I know that you're nice and fun, too. I can't wait to hang out with you again!

Andrew

Love-Set-Match

Isn't that the sweetest thing you've ever heard?

"Let me see it," Allison said. But Coach Worth blew his whistle. "Girls! You won't beat Ravenwood by standing around gossiping!"

I promised to show Allison the letter later. I quickly folded it up and stuffed it in my pocket.

Coach Worth came over to work with Allison and me on our serves.

"Bend your legs more, Ashley," Coach said. "The real power comes from your legs, not your arms."

I served over and over, trying to get it right. On the next court, Max was actually beating Andrew, even though Andrew is a way better player. Every time Andrew missed a shot, the coach scowled.

Finally, Andrew hit three serves in a row into the net. Coach lost his temper.

"I've seen enough, Andrew," he growled. "Take three laps around the courts. I hope I never see you play this badly again."

Andrew glanced at me and grinned. It was as if he didn't even care that his dad just yelled at him!

I quickly looked away. Andrew's mind wasn't on his game at all. I just hope the coach won't figure out why!

Dear Diary,
    I don't know what to do about

49

Jessie! She's been following me around everywhere!

I told her I'd play with her after lunch during our free period. So at lunchtime I was sitting by myself, waiting for Ashley to show up, and Patrick came in! He sat next to me. Ashley and Allison came in a few minutes later, but when they saw me and Patrick sitting together, they just waved to us and sat at another table.

Patrick was so nice! "You were making great time on the wilderness course today," he said.

"I *was*," I said. "Until my little accident."

"That could have happened to anyone," he said.

Sure, I thought. *Anyone who has Jessie as a Little Sister.*

He started teasing me. "I heard they're adding a new competition to the Camp Games this year," he said. "It's called the Dirtball Challenge. Whoever gets muddiest wins."

"Very funny," I said, but I laughed.

Then Jessie walked up to us. She was wearing my pink hairclip – it still makes her hair stick out everywhere – and carrying  a tray with three peanut butter sandwiches and a carton of milk on it. She tugged on Patrick's sleeve.

"You're in my spot," she said. Then she got between us and actually shoved Patrick over! She squeezed in next to me.

"Mary-Kate needs to sit next to me," she told Patrick.

"Jessie, I told you I'd come play with you after lunch," I said. "Don't you want to go sit with the other girls in your bunk?"

"No," Jessie said. "I don't like them." She turned to Patrick and added, "You can go away now."

"Patrick, you don't have to go anywhere," I said.

But Patrick stood and picked up his tray. "That's okay. I'll go sit with Jason and Mindy. See you later, Mary-Kate."

"Jessie!" I cried. I wanted to scream! But what could I say? I'm her Big Sister. I'm supposed to be there for her.

So the two of us ate lunch together, which was kind of gross. She sneezed and milk came out of her nose.

But then we went to get an ice cream cone from a soft-serve machine that was set up in the mess hall. By the time Jessie was through she had chocolate all over her face. I couldn't help it, Diary. I started to laugh. After lunch we got Jessie cleaned up and went for a walk. We had fun. I guess I can't stay mad at her for long.

"I want to show you my favourite tree," she said. She dragged me though the woods, stopping and staring at different trees. Finally she stopped at a giant old oak near the lake.

"Here it is!" she cried. There was a big hollow in the trunk. Jessie stepped inside. "Look!" she shouted. "I can hide in here! Come on in – there's room for you, too, Mary-Kate!"

I stuck my head inside the hollow. "I don't think I can fit," I said. "But it's perfect for you."

I glanced at my watch. "Come on out now. It's time for you to go back to your cabin. You have canoeing in ten minutes. "

She popped out and followed me back to the little girls' cabins. My bunk had crafts in an hour. I decided to head back to the cabin to rest. But Claire pulled me into a pickup volleyball game. The score was tied, and I was just about to spike the winning

volley over the net – when somebody dove in front of me and I tripped! Oof! I tumbled to the ground.

I sat up. It was Jessie. Again! Claire was furious. She hates to lose.

"What is she doing here?" Claire asked.

I turned to Jessie and waited for an answer.

"I was helping you win the game!" Jessie said.

"But why aren't you back at your cabin, where you're supposed to be?" I asked her.

"I told Lisa I was thirsty," she explained. "She said I could go get a drink of water if I came right back."

I just shook my head and sent her back to her cabin. At dinner tonight I sat with Ashley and told her the whole story.

"I'm Jessie's Big Sister," I said. "I'm supposed to be with her and help her out. But she's always around – and she always causes trouble!"

"Why don't you talk to Nancy? Maybe she can give you some advice," Ashley suggested.

That's exactly what I did. I stopped by the camp director's office and knocked on her door. "Nancy? Can I talk to you for a minute?" I asked, and then I told her my problem.

Nancy frowned. "Have you talked to her counsellor about the sneaking away?" she asked.

"No," I said. I didn't want to tell Nancy that Jessie's counsellor knew about it. I didn't want to get the girl in trouble.

"Well, I've noticed that you've formed a real bond with Jessie," Nancy said. "But you don't have to spend all your time with her. Would you like me to explain to her that you need your own time?"

I wasn't sure. "I just feel bad for her," I said. "Jessie doesn't have any friends her own age." Then I stopped. "Wait. Maybe that's the answer! I can help Jessie find some friends her own age."

"That's not a bad idea," Nancy replied, "if you're willing to put in the work."

"Why not?" I shrugged. "Jessie will be happier and she won't pester me as much. Thanks, Nancy!"

I planned to go find Jessie right after that, but of course, I didn't have to bother. She found me.

"Can I hang out at your cabin?" she asked.

"Why don't we go to the playground?" I suggested. "We can play on the swings."

"Okay." She seemed to like that idea.

At the playground I spotted two little girls Jessie's age. They were playing with their dolls on a big tree stump.

"Do you know those girls?" I asked Jessie.

She nodded. "That's Sarah and Jasmine."

"Let's see if they want to play," I said. I led Jessie over to them.

"Hi, girls," I said. "What are you doing?"

"We're playing princess," Sarah said, showing us her doll. "This is her castle." She pointed to the stump.

"Can Jessie play with you?" I asked.

Sarah and Jasmine looked at each other. "Does she have a doll?" Sarah asked.

I looked at Jessie. "Yeah, I have a doll," she said.

Jasmine shrugged. "Okay, you can play with us."

"Go get your doll, Jessie," I said.

Jessie ran into her cabin. *This is working out great!* I thought. *If they just give Jessie a chance, I'm sure they'll all be friends.*

Jessie returned with her doll – but it was no princess. It was a G.I. Joe dressed for battle. And he came with his own helicopter.

"Look out, princesses, here I come!" Jessie shouted. She stuck her doll in the helicopter and flew him over the tree-stump "castle."

Jasmine wrinkled her nose. "What's that?"

"He's the prince," Jessie declared. "He's coming to take over the castle."

"We don't want him to take over the castle," Sarah said. "We want him to go to the ball. But he has to change his clothes first."

"But he can't go to the ball!" Jessie shouted. "The ball is cancelled. Because a terrible dragon is eating everybody!"

She roared, pretending to be the dragon. She stomped around the tree stump, growling. Then she picked up Sarah's doll and tried to bite off its head!

"Stop it!" Sarah screamed. She snatched the doll away from Jessie.

"I'm playing castle!" Jessie said. "Castles have dragons!"

Sarah clutched her doll and glared at Jessie. Jasmine picked up her doll.

"You can't play with us," Sarah said. She and Jasmine walked away.

"Wait," I called after them. "Jessie was just pretending!"

But they kept walking. Jessie looked up at me with her big, dark eyes. "Did I do something wrong?" she asked. "When I play castle with my brothers, there's always a dragon."

I gave her a hug. What could I tell her? "Even if you're pretending to be a dragon, you shouldn't bite other people's dolls," I told her. "But don't worry. We'll find somebody for you to play with."

"I don't need anybody to play with," Jessie said. "I have you!"

My heart sank. This Big Sister stuff was turning out to be a lot harder than I thought.

Chapter 7

Thursday

Dear Diary,

We had another competition against Ravenwood today. After breakfast, instead of morning swim, we had a swim meet against Ravenwood in Lake Evergreen. At least, that's what we call it. *They* call it Ravenwood Lake!

I guess they have the right to call it whatever they want, because they creamed us! Andrew said they were good at water sports, and he was right.

So now the score in the Camp Games is two to nothing, and we're losing!

"We can't let them do this to us," Claire said as we trudged back to our cabin. "We've got to shut Ravenwood down – now!"

"Let's get that portrait tonight," Allison said.

"Tonight will be perfect," Mindy said. "All the signs are good."

"Tonight?" Emily asked. "You mean after dark? In the woods? Isn't that kind of scary?"

"Don't worry," I said. "We'll all be together."

"There's no other way," Mary-Kate added. "We have to do it for the honour of Camp Evergreen!"

Andrew ran up to me just as we got to our cabin. "Hey, Ashley," he said. "We've got a few minutes before tennis practice. Want to take a walk with me?"

"Sure," I said. I could feel all the other girls staring at us and trying not to giggle. "Let me just put on my tennis clothes and I'll be right out."

I hurried into the cabin to change. "Wow, he really likes you," Mindy whispered. "What sign is he?"

"I don't know," I said. "But whatever it is, it goes pretty well with Gemini."

I left the cabin with my racquet and found Andrew waiting on the path.

"Have you been to Martha's Meadow?" he asked.

"No," I said. "I haven't even heard of it."

He took my hand. "Come on, I'll show it to you."

He led me down the trail, past all the cabins, past the playing field, past the wilderness course, to the edge of Camp Evergreen. There was a beautiful meadow filled with yellow wildflowers.

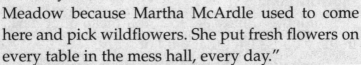

"It's so pretty!" I gasped.

"They call it Martha's Meadow because Martha McArdle used to come here and pick wildflowers. She put fresh flowers on every table in the mess hall, every day."

I waded into the field, picking brightly-coloured flowers as I went. Andrew flopped onto the grass and stared at the sky. He grabbed a handful of flowers and placed them on his head. "So how do I look?" He stuck out his tongue and crossed his eyes.

"Stupid," I said, laughing. I brushed the flowers from his head.

I sighed. "We have to beat Ravenwood in the tennis tournament," I said. Then I decided to ask Andrew something.

"Andrew," I began, "I was wondering . . ."

"Yeah?" he said.

"Well, you weren't playing so well at practice yesterday," I said a little nervously. I didn't want him to take this the wrong way.

He sighed. "I know. Believe me, Dad never let me hear the end of it."

"What happened?" I asked. "Did it have something to do with me?"

He sat up. "Don't worry about it, Ashley," he said. "I'm allowed to miss a few tennis shots once in a while, right? It's no big deal."

"I just don't want to cause any trouble between you and your dad," I said. Then I noticed the watch on his wrist. "Oops! We're going to be late for practice!"

We grabbed our racquets and raced out of the meadow. We arrived at the courts, out of breath. Tennis practice had already started. Coach Worth glared at us. Then he looked at the flowers in my hand.

Uh-oh.

"Where have you two been?" he demanded.

"Sorry we're late, Dad," Andrew said. "We lost track of the time."

"It won't happen again," I promised.

"I know it won't," Coach Worth said. "Because if it does, you're both off the team! Now give me three laps around the courts, both of you. And then let's get some practice in before the morning is over!"

Andrew and I ran our laps. I hardly dared to look at the coach. He was *mad*.

And he was on us the whole rest of practice. "Keep those legs bent when you serve, Ashley!" he shouted at me three different times.

"That's a racquet, not a fly swatter!" he yelled at Andrew. "Put some power into it!"

I got so nervous that I started missing easy shots. "Wake up, Sleeping Beauty!" Coach called.

Finally, Andrew cracked. "Listen, Dad," he said. "You can pick on me all you want. But stop picking on Ashley. She didn't do anything wrong!"

I held my breath. What was Andrew doing? I couldn't believe he was fighting with his dad about me. I wanted to melt into the tennis court.

Coach Worth's face turned red. "This is my team," he said. "If you're going to be on it, you'll play by my rules."

"Fine!" Andrew said. "Then I quit!" He threw down his racquet and stormed off the court.

I gasped. Andrew's off the tennis team? How will we ever beat Ravenwood without him?

I glanced around at my teammates. They all looked really upset. I think I caught a few of them glaring at me.

Which means only one thing. I have to find a way to get Andrew back on the team – and soon!

Dear Diary,

Well, tonight was the night.

"Is it time yet?" Claire asked impatiently.

"Five more minutes," Mindy said. "The moon has to line up perfectly with the North Star—"

"Oh, come on!" Claire snapped. "Let's just go!"

Mindy crossed her arms over her chest. "Fine. Go ahead. But if we get caught, you'll know why."

Claire rolled her eyes. "Oh, brother."

"I'm getting sleepy," Emily complained.

It was very late – almost midnight! But we wanted everything to be perfect when we sneaked over to Camp Ravenwood to steal the painting.

Two of a Kind Diaries

Well, we weren't really sneaking. We told Jill our plan, and she promised to "look the other way" as long as we were back in an hour.

Finally Mindy went outside and checked the sky. "Okay, we can go now," she said.

I was the first one out the door. Patrick and Jason were meeting us by the fork in the trail. I hurried down the trail, flashlight in hand. All of a sudden – "Boo!" Someone jumped out in front of me!

I muffled a scream and aimed my flashlight on the person. It was a very short person.

"Jessie!" I whispered. "You should have been in bed hours ago!"

"I can't sleep," she complained. "The moon's too bright. Where are you going?"

"Nowhere. Now get back to your cabin."

My cabin mates caught up with me. "Is that Jessie?" Allison asked. "What's she doing here?"

"I know where you're going," Jessie said. "To steal that picture! Right?"

I didn't know what to say. I didn't want to lie to her. After all, I'm her Big Sister, and I'm supposed to set a good example. But I didn't want her to come with us.

"We've got to hurry," Mindy said. "Once the planets shift, we'll lose our good luck."

"You *are* going to Ravenwood!" Jessie cried.

"Can I come with you, Mary-Kate? Please, please?"

"No," I said. "You're supposed to be in bed!"

"Let her tag along," Claire snapped. "We don't have time to argue with her."

I sighed and took Jessie's hand.

"Hurray!" she cheered.

"Shhh!" I hushed her. "You'll wake everybody up!"

We continued down the trail until we came to the fork. Patrick and Jason were waiting for us there.

"Hey," Patrick said to me. "What's Jessie doing here?"

"She decided to tag along," I told him.

We walked quietly down the trail, leaving Camp Evergreen behind. Up ahead we could see the glowing lights of Camp Ravenwood.

Jessie tugged on my sleeve. "Mary-Kate," she said. "I have to go to the bathroom."

"What?" I said. "Now?"

"Yes," she said. "Right now."

"Well, okay," I said. "You can go over there, behind that rock."

Jessie shook her head. "Out here? In the dark? What if a snake bites me?"

"That won't happen," I told her.

"Take me to the bathhouse at camp," she insisted. "Please, Mary-Kate. It's an emergency!"

"We can't go back to camp," Mindy warned. "It will ruin our auras!"

"Mary-Kate!" Jessie whined. "Hurry!"

I held my breath and counted to five before speaking. Jessie was really annoying me, and I didn't want to say anything I would regret. But what I had to do was obvious. I couldn't let Jessie ruin the whole group's aura. "I'll take Jessie to the bathroom. You all go on without me."

I turned around and headed back to camp with Jessie. I couldn't believe this. I could never get away from her – not even in the middle of the night!

I took Jessie to the bathhouse and she went to the bathroom. "Let's go find the others," she said.

"No way," I said. "I'm taking you back to your cabin right now."

I practically had to drag her towards the little girls' cabins. We were almost there, when a shadow crossed our paths.

"Girls, what are you doing out at this hour?" a stern voice said.

A flashlight shined on me. I turned to look. It was Nancy Grable, the camp director!

Oh, no. I was in for it now.

Chapter 8

Thursday

Dear Diary,

I had to think fast. I hardly knew what was coming out of my mouth. I just started talking.

Nancy stared at us. She shone her flashlight in my face, then in Jessie's.

"I'm really sorry, Nancy," I said. "I know it's after curfew. Jessie couldn't sleep, and she came out looking for me. I knew she should go right back to bed, but I didn't want her to walk back alone. So I'm taking her back to her cabin right now."

Nancy stared at us. Then her face relaxed. She bought it.

"I'm glad you're looking out for her," she said. "Jessie, you don't go out after dark alone any more, you hear me?"

"Yes," Jessie said.

"All right," Nancy said. "Mary-Kate, take Jessie back to her cabin, and then go straight to bed."

"I will," I promised.

Nancy went on her way. I hurried Jessie back to her cabin.

I paused at Jessie's cabin door, feeling guilty. I hadn't exactly lied to Nancy, but I hadn't told her

65

the whole truth, either. I was afraid of setting a bad example for my Little Sister. "Jessie, you know that lying is wrong, don't you?" I asked her.

She nodded. "Yup."

"Good. So from now on, you should always tell the truth," I said. "And I will, too."

"Okay," she said. She opened the door of her cabin. Her bunk mates and her counsellor, Lisa, were all sleeping. I didn't see any reason to wake them up. So I put Jessie to bed and tucked her in.

Then I hurried back towards my cabin. I heard whispering on the trail. I hid, waiting to see who it was.

"This is disgusting!" someone whispered.

That was Ashley's voice! I came out and shone my light on them. Ashley, Jason, Patrick and all my bunk mates stood before me, covered in slime!

"What happened?" I asked.

"The Ravenwood campers were ready for us," Patrick said. "They must have posted a lookout."

"They saw us coming and threw eggs at us!" Ashley said.

"We never even got close to the portrait," Allison added.

"Our timing was off," Mindy said. "That Little Sister of yours made us lose precious minutes."

"It's not Mary-Kate's fault," Patrick said. "She couldn't help it if Jessie had to go to the bathroom."

"Jessie never should have tagged along with us," Allison said. "I know little kids, Mary-Kate. You have to lay down the rules, or they'll do whatever they want!"

I knew Allison was right. I had to get Jessie under control. But I guess I shouldn't be too angry with her. After all, she saved me from getting egged!

Dear Diary,

I went looking for Andrew as soon as I entered the mess hall this morning. I found him in the cold-breakfast line.

"Hey, Ashley," he said. He grabbed some cereal and milk and set them on his tray. I took a large orange juice.

"Better get something to eat," Andrew said. "You need your strength for tennis practice."

"What are you going to do this morning?" I asked him.

"I thought I'd join the boys' singing group," he said. "Ah ah ah ah!" he sang in an off-key croak.

"Very funny," I said.

We went to a table and sat down. "Andrew, you're crazy. You can't quit the tennis team. We need you!"

"No, you don't," he said. "You can beat Ravenwood without me. And besides, if the team needs me so much, my dad wouldn't have let me go so easily. He hates to lose."

"Come on. You're the one who quit!" I said. "I know it's probably hard to have your dad for a coach, but we need you! Do you know what happened last night?"

He laughed. "Yeah, I heard all about it from Patrick. You got egged!"

"That's right," I said. "It's not going to be easy stealing that portrait. So we can't take any chances. We can't let Ravenwood beat us again! If you come back to the tennis team, we can't lose!"

"I want to come back, but my dad drives me nuts," Andrew complained. "And I know he's going to say I have to focus only on tennis. He might even tell me I can't hang out with you anymore."

I gulped. I knew that was a possibility, but I wanted to stay positive. "He won't do that," I said. "Besides, all of Evergreen needs you."

He chewed his cornflakes. Then he looked at me and sighed. "It means that much to you?" he asked.

I nodded.

"Okay. Then I'll come back," he agreed. "But," he added, "if my dad says I can't hang with you any more, I'm gonna say forget it."

We finished breakfast, and I went to morning swim. (You know, I thought I would hate morning swim, but I've actually got a nice tan from it!) Then I changed and head-ed for tennis. I didn't dare come late to practice again, so this time I was early.

Still, most of the team was on the courts when I got there. I guess they were all afraid to be late.

Then Andrew strolled onto the court.

"Just a minute, son," Coach Worth said. "I thought you quit."

"I changed my mind," Andrew said.

Coach Worth folded his arms across his chest. "I don't think so."

What? My eyes almost bugged out of my head.

"But, Dad, you have to let me back on the team," Andrew said.

"I don't have to do anything," Coach replied.

"Please, Coach, we need him." Max stood up. "He's our best player."

"We have a real chance of winning this year," Allison said.

I glanced at the coach. His face was starting to soften. I knew that would get him.

"Look, I'm sorry for quitting. I got mad. I won't lose it again – I promise."

Coach Worth frowned. "Come with me," he said. He took Andrew aside to talk to him. But everyone could hear what they were saying.

"I'd like to have you back," Coach said. "But there's going to be no more fooling around. You can come back on one condition."

"What?" Andrew asked.

"You need to keep your mind on tennis," Coach Worth said. "Practise all the time. Eat, sleep and breathe tennis. That means you can no longer hang out with Ashley."

I winced. Max mouthed the word "ouch."

I could feel everybody watching and listening.

I was totally embarrassed. And my spirits sagged. Our team was ruined! I knew there was no way Andrew would ever agree not to see me.

Then Andrew said, "Okay. I won't see her any more."

Chapter 9

Friday

Dear Diary,

Andrew Worth is a total liar. He said he wasn't going to dump me, and he did. And you know what, Diary? I wouldn't have been so mad at him if he hadn't done it in front of the ENTIRE TEAM!

And then he had the nerve to turn to me and say, "Sorry, Ashley. The team really needs me."

"The team needs me"! What about how he promised he wouldn't stop seeing me? I was totally humiliated!

"Come on, Ashley," Max said. "Let's play a practice match." He dragged me off to the last court, far away from Andrew and his dad.

I squared off at the service line and whacked the best serve of my life over to Max.

Every time the ball came to me, I drove it back to Max's side of the court.

I played my best game ever. You know why? Because I was pretending the ball was Andrew's head!

Who does he think he is? I thought angrily. WHACK!

I hope he loses every game he ever plays for the rest of his life! WHACK! *And I'm never going to speak to him again – except maybe to tell him that I'm never going to speak to him again!* WHACK!

"Whoa!" Max cried as one of my shots whizzed by him. He pulled his white bandanna off his head and waved it in the air. "I surrender!"

"Way to go, Ashley!" Allison cheered. She and my other teammates gathered around to congratulate me. It felt good to play so well. Really good.

Maybe tennis is turning out to be my thing, Diary. If I work a little harder at it, I could be pretty good. Just like Andrew said . . . no, I've got to erase him from my mind.

But I promise to practise a lot. I'm going to help Evergreen beat Ravenwood! We don't need that big creep Andrew. We can do it without him. *WHACK!*

Dear Diary,

I had the best idea to find Jessie some friends her age. She doesn't fit in with the other girls – because she's too much like a boy. So maybe she should be friends with the boys!

After my crafts class I picked up Jessie at her cabin and we went over by the lake to hang out. She was still wearing that hair clip.

We saw five boys about her age near the lake, playing hide-and-seek. Jessie and I watched them for a few minutes. I could tell she wanted to play with them. So I said, "Go on, Jessie. Go ask them if you can play, too."

It took a little push, but she went over and asked.

The biggest boy, kind of the leader, stared at her suspiciously. "We don't play with girls."

"Jessie's a very good player," I told them. "And she doesn't mind being It. Do you, Jess?"

She shook her head. "I like being It."

"Well, okay," the boy said.

Yes! I thought. *It's working!*

The boy told us his name was Nicky, and the other boys were Ralph, Marcus, Danny and Sam.

Jessie covered her eyes and started counting to twenty. The boys hid. Jessie shouted, "Ready or not, here I come!" and spotted Sam right away. She ran over to the tree where he was hiding and shoved him. "You're It!" she shouted.

Sam toppled over. "Ow!" he cried.

Now Sam was It. He couldn't catch Jessie. None of the boys could. She was too fast for them. I could tell they didn't like that – especially Nicky.

Finally, she tripped and Ralph caught her. She was It again. But after counting to twenty, she ran over to Marcus and tackled him!

"Hey!" Marcus cried, rubbing his arm.

"You're It!" she shrieked, waving her hands in

the air. I could see that she was getting over-excited.

I put one hand on my forehead. I could tell this was going to a bad place.

"We don't want to play any more," Nicky said.

"Why?" Jessie asked. "I'm having fun."

"Well, we're not," Nicky said. "I knew we shouldn't play with a girl."

The boys left Jessie standing alone in the field. I called her over.

"Why did they leave?" she asked.

"Well," I began, "maybe you shouldn't play so rough. You might have hurt one of them."

"I was just trying to win," Jessie said. "Should I let them win?"

"No, that's not the answer," I said. But I realised I didn't know what the answer was.

The girls won't play with her. The boys won't play with her. What am I going to do now?

Dear Diary,

I had to write in you again today. Something terrible happened tonight. Guess whose fault it was.

Of course. Jessie's!

I know she doesn't mean to keep getting in the way, but she does. Here's what happened. We decided to make another raid on Ravenwood.

Mindy checked her charts. We were all set to go.

We gathered the troops tonight at ten-thirty – Tree Frogs plus Jason and Patrick. We sneaked over to Ravenwood without getting caught by Nancy. We made it all the way to the Ravenwood lodge.

We huddled outside, ready to strike. I sneaked up to the window and peeked inside.

Uh-oh. Six Ravenwood campers – including Shawna, Pete, Lindsay, and Rob – were sleeping on the floor inside the lodge.

"We've got trouble," I reported back to the group. "Guards!"

"What are we going to do?" Ashley said.

Something crackled in the woods behind us. We froze. There was another noise. We stared at the woods, waiting to see what would come out into the moonlight. Was it a counsellor? A bear?

No. It was Jessie.

I should have known!

"Jessie, what are you doing here?" I whispered. "You shouldn't be out wandering through the woods at night!"

"I wasn't wandering," she said. "I was following you."

All the others frowned at me. "Mary-Kate, you have to do something about her," Allison said.

"I'm trying!" I replied, but inside I was glad

Jessie hadn't got hurt following us. This was really getting out of hand.

"Just keep her quiet!" Claire snapped.

Jessie crept up to the window and peeked through. "Jessie, come back here!" I hissed.

She hurried back. "I have an idea," she said.

"Shhh," I said. "We're making a plan."

"LISTEN TO ME!" Jessie shouted.

I clapped a hand over Jessie's mouth. But it was too late. The guards heard us – and they were awake!

"Somebody's out there!" Shawna shouted.

"Run!" Ashley cried.

We scrambled into to the woods and ran all the way home. I glanced back to see if anyone followed us. But they must have been too sleepy or too lazy.

"You should have listened to me," Jessie said when we were safely at camp. "I had a great idea."

"What was it?" I asked.

"Sneak in on our tippy toes," she said. "That way the guards won't wake up!"

"Yeah – good thinking," I said.

Another plan ruined, thanks to you-know-who!

Chapter 10

Saturday

Dear Diary,

I can't believe we missed getting the portrait – again! Everybody was furious with Jessie. She's always in the way! I don't know how Mary-Kate stops herself from yelling at her.

We tried to be quiet once we got back to Evergreen, so Nancy or one of the counsellors wouldn't catch us out after lights-out. Mary-Kate was taking Jessie back to her cabin, but first she had to pass by ours.

We left Patrick and Jason at the fork in the trail and crept up to Tree Frogs. In the moonlight we could see a shadow. Someone was standing outside our cabin!

"Oh, no," Claire whispered. "What if it's Nancy? We're dead!"

I stared at the shadow. There was something familiar about it. We went a little closer.

Then I knew who it was. Andrew. What did *he* want?

"Hey – that's Ashley's boyfriend!" Jessie said.

Mary-Kate hurried her away. "Time for you to go back to bed, Jessie," she said, gripping her hand.

My other bunk mates went inside the cabin. I

started for the door, too, but Andrew stopped me.

"I've got to get some sleep," I told him. I really didn't care what he had to say to me.

"Ashley, you don't understand," he said. "I still want to see you!"

I stopped. "Then why did you promise your dad you wouldn't see me anymore?" I demanded. "You humiliated me in front of everybody!"

Andrew winced. "I know. I'm so sorry," he said. "But what else could I say? If I didn't, he wouldn't let me back on the team. You wanted me back on the team, right?"

"I really don't care any more," I said. But deep down, I did want Andrew to be on the team. I knew we couldn't win without him.

"I didn't mean it," he insisted. "I was just faking him out. We can still see each other. We just have to keep it a secret."

A secret? I wasn't sure this was such a good idea. Coach Worth wanted Andrew to do nothing but play tennis. If he found out about us, we could both be off the team! Plus, I wasn't so sure I was ready to forgive him.

"It could be kind of like Romeo and Juliet," Andrew added. He fell down on one knee and spread his arms. "My dad won't let us be together – but nothing can keep us apart! Not even tennis!"

I giggled. Andrew was so funny. Plus I love the story of Romeo and Juliet. . .

"All right," I agreed. "We can see each other again – in secret."

He stood up and kissed me on the cheek.

"But we'd better get some sleep now," I added. "We've got practice in the morning."

He walked down the path. I went into the cabin to get ready for bed. My bunk mates were lying in their beds with their eyes closed, pretending to be asleep.

"Come on, guys," I said. "I know you heard every word."

Allison sat up. She hadn't even changed into her pyjamas yet. "Don't worry." She grinned. "We'll keep your secret."

I swear, Diary. There is no privacy in this camp.

Dear Diary,

Today is the Wilderness Challenge! I'm a little nervous. I've been training hard, and Patrick and I went on an extra run this morning. But I haven't seen

Ravenwood's team. I have no idea how good they are.

After my run I stopped by the tennis courts to watch Ashley practise. The session was almost over. Allison quit for the day and sat beside me on the bench.

"I'm so tired today," she said. "We stayed up late two nights in a row – and we still don't have the portrait!"

I sighed. "I'm sorry about Jessie."

"You've got to do something about her," Allison said.

"I know," I said. "But what?"

"Be firm," Allison said. "That's how I act with my brothers and sisters."

That's what Nancy said, I remembered. "I thought I *was* being firm," I told Allison. "I guess I'll just have to be even firmer."

"Look who it is," Allison said. Jessie was walking towards us. She sat down on the bench beside me. Allison stood up. "See you later," she said.

Across the court, Ashley was wiping her face with a towel. "See you at crafts!" she called to me. Then she left with Allison. Andrew stayed behind to volley with his dad.

"Jessie, where are your cabin mates?" I asked her. "What activity do you have now?"

Jessie shrugged. "I don't know. Lisa was walking us somewhere, and I saw you. So I just sneaked away."

"Again? She's going to wonder where you are," I said. I decided to lay down the law right then and there.

"Jessie, listen," I began. "You have to stop following me around. I like spending time with you, but—"

Just then a ball bounced right at me. I caught it and Coach Worth came over to get it.

"Nice catch," he said, looking carefully at me. "You must be Ashley's sister."

I nodded.

"I've heard you're a good athlete," he went on. "Ever think about joining the tennis team?"

"I'm doing the Wilderness Challenge," I told him. "And some other activities—"

"She's my Big Sister," Jessie added.

"Anyway, you have a great team without me," I finished.

"They're getting better," Coach Worth said. "Especially Andrew and Ashley. Now that they're more focused on tennis—"

"We saw Andrew last night," Jessie said. "He's Ashley's boyfriend."

81

Coach Worth turned red. "What?"

"Jessie!" I said. But it was too late.

"Andrew sneaked out to meet Ashley at her cabin," Jessie added.

"I don't believe this!" the coach roared.

I clapped my hand over Jessie's mouth. "She doesn't know what she's talking about," I said. "She likes to make things up, you know, play pretend."

But Coach Worth didn't buy it. It didn't matter what I said – he knew the truth. And he didn't look happy about it!

Chapter 11

Sunday

Dear Diary,

My summer is ruined.

I was supposed to meet Andrew at the mess hall for lunch this afternoon, but he never showed up. So I decided to go to his cabin and see what was up.

The door was open a crack. I pushed it open and saw Andrew sitting on his bunk with his head in his hands. Max was sitting next to him. They both looked totally bummed.

"Andrew," I said, "what's going on?"

Max looked up. "See you later," he said, and left.

I sat down beside Andrew. "What is it?" I asked. "Are you all right?"

"Bad news," Andrew told me. "My dad found out about us."

"No!" I exclaimed. "How?"

"Jessie told him," Andrew said.

"Jessie? But—" Then I remembered seeing Jessie sitting with Mary-Kate at the tennis courts this morning. And Jessie saw Andrew waiting for me last night.

"I'm sure we can fix this," I said. "Everyone knows Jessie does stuff to get attention. Maybe if Mary-Kate talks to your dad—"

Andrew shook his head. "It's too late. Dad is furious." He paused. "He's sending me home," he finished.

"What?" I gasped.

"I'm supposed to leave at the end of the week," he added.

"No!" I was stunned. Things were going so well. And now they're all falling apart!

"But what about tennis?" I asked.

"Dad says I'll be more focused on tennis at home," he said. "I'll work with my regular coach without any distractions. I'll be able to spend *all* my time on tennis. Great."

Diary, I'm crushed! If Andrew leaves . . . I might never see him again!

Dear Diary,

I had a feeling Ashley wasn't going to be in a good mood this afternoon after what happened with Coach Worth.

I was right. She stormed into the mess hall when lunch was almost over. I could tell by the look on her face that she was mad.

"Coach Worth is sending Andrew home!" she told me. "And it's all because of Jessie!"

Oh, no! I knew Coach Worth was upset. But I didn't

think he'd go that far! I couldn't help it, Diary. But at that moment I really didn't like Jessie at all!

"I'm going to talk to Jessie right now," I promised. "And don't worry, Ashley. We'll find a way to change the coach's mind."

"I hope so," Ashley said miserably.

I ran to the little kids' area to find Jessie. She was sitting by herself on the seesaw, bouncing up and down while some other girls played in the sandbox.

"Jessie, I need to talk to you," I said. I took her by the hand and led her to a bench. "Sit down."

She sat down. For once she was quiet. She looked scared.

"You did a very bad thing, Jessie," I scolded her. "Why did you tell on Andrew and Ashley? You got them in big trouble!"

"What do you mean?" Jessie asked.

"Andrew wasn't supposed to see Ashley," I said. "Now his dad is sending him home! And it's all because of what you said!"

"But you told me to say it," Jessie said.

"What? I never told you to do anything like that."

"Yes, you did," Jessie insisted. "You told me to always tell the truth."

I paused. I did say that. "But this is different," I said.

"Why?" she asked.

"It just is," I said. I was losing patience with her. "Listen, Jessie, you can't keep hanging around with me all the time. You need some friends your own age. And you need to stay with your cabin! No more sneaking away. No more bothering me. We can see each other three hours a week, but that's it!"

Jessie's eyes pooled with tears. "I thought you were my friend." She sniffled. "Why are you being so mean to me?"

"Jessie—" I began, but she ran off.

Her counsellor, Lisa, ran after her. I sighed. Maybe this is for the best. I didn't want to hurt her feelings – but she just wasn't getting the message!

I think I've done the right thing. But why do I feel so bad?

Chapter 12

Monday

Dear Diary,

So much happened today! This afternoon was the Wilderness Challenge. It was held in the middle of the woods between Evergreen and Ravenwood. I couldn't believe how many people came to see it! It seemed like everyone from both camps was there.

Except Jessie. I didn't see her anywhere. And it was kind of weird. I'm so used to her popping up all the time.

But I didn't have time to think about that. I had to focus on the race! I promised myself I'd look for Jessie when it was over.

Patrick stood beside me at the starting line, shaking out his legs. "Good luck, Mary-Kate," he said.

"Good luck to you, too," I said. "May the best team win – Evergreen!"

We lined up to start. The race was a relay. Each team had five racers. Patrick was third, and I was going last.

Oh, no, I thought as I looked over Ravenwood's line-up. *I'm going to have to run against that mean girl Shawna!*

The whistle blew. And they were off!

"Go, Evergreen!" I shouted as our first runner shot onto the course. We were doing well, but

Ravenwood's team was very good. By the time Patrick's turn came, we were about even with them.

"Go, Patrick!" I yelled. Patrick made great time. He pulled ahead of his Ravenwood rival. When my turn came, we were in the lead!

Don't blow it, I told myself. I ran to the tree and scrambled up as fast as I could. Shawna was right behind me.

I stumbled across the rope bridge, trying not to think about how high it was. *Don't think. Just go!* I told myself.

But my foot slipped. The crowd gasped as I fell to my knees on the bridge. I quickly stood up and scurried over the ropes. But Shawna had pulled ahead of me!

I grabbed the next rope and slid down it as fast as I could. Then I ran hard, dodging rocks and logs, until I came to the spider's web. Shawna was almost finished with it. But I zipped across it as if I had eight legs. I was so close, I could almost touch her!

Shawna reached the stream and swung across with a Tarzan yell. But I was right behind her. I glided over the water and landed neatly on the other side – just behind Shawna.

Dig deep, I told myself. *You can do it! You can beat her!*

It was the final stretch – just a run through the

mud to the finish line. I dug my heels into the dirt and sprinted. I gave it everything I had. Shawna and I were neck and neck.

Don't let her beat you! I thought. *Ravenwood can't win!*

With a final surge of energy I bolted across the finish line – just ahead of Shawna!

"Evergreen wins!" the referee called. The crowd went crazy! Everybody was jumping up and down and screaming.

Patrick threw his arms around me. We hopped up and down, hugging and laughing. "We won! We won!" he shouted.

Then he suddenly let me go – as if he just realised what he was doing. He looked embarrassed. "Uh, way to go, Mary-Kate," he said, slapping my hand.

Ashley and all my cabin mates swarmed around us, cheering. "All right!" Ashley shouted. "We finally beat Ravenwood! The score is two to one now!"

One part of me felt really happy. But the other part felt really bad. I scanned the crowd, looking for Jessie, but there was no sign of her.

I totally hurt her feelings, I thought as a pang of guilt shot through me.

I knew what I had to do. I had to go find Jessie – and make it up to her.

89

Two of a Kind Diaries

Dear Diary,

Hurray for Mary-Kate! She really saved the day in the Wilderness Challenge. Now we're not so far behind Ravenwood. We decided to go after the portrait one more time.

And this time Andrew came with us. He figured he had nothing to lose – he's going home anyway. I was glad to have a little more time to be with him.

So after dark we sneaked through the woods. No problem. Jessie didn't show up, either, which helped. But Mary-Kate was worried about her. She hadn't seen Jessie all day.

We tiptoed up to the lodge and peeked inside. The portrait was still hanging over the fireplace. And three kids – Pete, Shawna and Rob – were sleeping underneath it, guarding it.

But we were ready for them. Andrew thought up a way to distract the guards. He squeezed my hand, then crept around the side of the lodge to put his plan into action.

The rest of us crouched against the wall of the building, waiting. Soon a soft moaning sound floated on the wind. "Ooooo . . . ooooooooooo . . ."

I covered my mouth and tried not to giggle. The moaning grew louder and louder. "Ooooooo . . . aaaaughgh . . ." It sounded like a tortured spirit. I never knew Andrew was so good at this!

The guards woke up. Rob sat up in his chair.

"Guys! Hey, guys!" he whispered. "Do you hear something?"

Pete and Shawna sat up groggily and looked around. "Ooooo . . ." Andrew moaned again.

"Something's out there!" Pete said.

"A ghost!" said Rob.

"That's not a ghost," Shawna said. "That's just some dude from Evergreen. They're after the portrait again."

"We'll go catch them and turn them in," Pete said to Rob. "You stay here and guard the portrait."

Pete and Shawna got up and left Rob alone. Then Andrew's voice came again – but this time from a different side of the building.

"Ohhhh . . . ohhhhh . . ."

Rob started to shake. "Hey! Wait for me!" he called after the other two. He burst out of the door and disappeared into the night.

Mary-Kate gave me the thumbs-up. Time to move in for the capture!

Chapter 13

Monday

Dear Diary,

We crawled in through the open window. The portrait was out of our reach. Patrick put Mary-Kate on his shoulders and boosted her up.

She grabbed the frame and lifted it off the nail on the wall. "Got it!" she whispered.

Patrick lowered her to the floor. "It's kind of heavy," she said. "Let's get this thing out of here!"

Patrick took the painting and we ran for the woods. I glanced back to see if anyone was following us. No sign of the Ravenwood kids. But where was Andrew?

We didn't stop running until we were back safely at Evergreen. "Woo-hoo!" we cheered in whispers. "We did it!"

Andrew came running out of the woods, gasping for breath.

"All right!" he panted. "You got it!"

"Did they follow you?" Emily asked, looking nervously toward the woods.

"They followed me at first," Andrew said. "In the opposite direction!" He laughed and tried to catch his breath. "I ran straight for their cabins – then I gave them the slip and ran the other way."

I threw my arms around Andrew and gave him a hug. We finally captured the portrait – thanks to Andrew's ghost!

We carried the picture all the way to our lodge and hung it over the fireplace.

"The whole camp will go crazy when they see this," Patrick said.

Mary-Kate laughed. "I can't wait for breakfast!"

"I'm not taking any chances," Claire said. "I'm going to sleep right here all night and guard this thing, just like they did."

"Me, too," Mindy said. "I'll go get our sleeping bags."

"Let's all spend the night here," Allison said.

"Sounds fun to me!" I cheered.

Everyone went to get sleeping bags. Andrew and I stayed in the lodge to guard the portrait until they came back.

He took my hand. "It's not fair," he said. "I'm having so much fun here at camp. And the best part is being with you."

He kissed me. I felt like melting into a puddle on the floor.

"It's not fair," I said. "You can't leave now. We have to find a way for you to stay. We just have to!"

Two of a Kind Diaries

Dear Diary,

The most awful thing has happened! Jessie has run away!

When I went back to the cabin with Patrick, Jason and the other girls, I saw something white lying on my bunk. A note. It was from Jessie!

It said (I fixed the misspellings):

Dear Mary-Kate,

I don't want to get in your way. Nobody likes me. So I'm running away. Forever.

Your ex-Little Sister,
Jessie

"Oh, no!" I cried. "This is terrible!" I showed the note to Patrick and the others.

"Maybe she's trying to get attention," Allison said.

"I hope so," I said. I felt as if someone had punched me in the stomach. "But what if she's really run away? I never should have told her not to hang around me so much. I hurt her feelings!"

"Let's go check her cabin," Patrick said. "I'll bet she's sleeping in her bunk right now."

I hurried out and raced toward Jessie's cabin. Patrick followed me.

Please let her be okay, I prayed.

Jessie's cabin was dark and quiet. I opened the door. Lisa, the counsellor, sat up. "Who's there?" she asked.

"It's me, Mary-Kate," I said. "Is Jessie here?"

"Sure," Lisa said. "She's right over there." She pointed to a lump on Jessie's bunk.

"She left me a note saying she was running away," I told Lisa. "So I had to check on her."

A couple of Jessie's bunk mates woke up. "What's going on?" one girl asked.

"Nothing," Lisa said. "Everything's okay. Go back to sleep."

I walked over to Jessie's bunk and pulled down the covers a little. "Oh, no!" I gasped. She wasn't there after all. It was only a pillow!

"She's gone!" I cried.

Lisa jumped to her feet and pulled on her jeans. "I'll go wake up Nancy," she said.

Diary, where could Jessie have gone? I thought of the dark woods, the twisting trails, the spooky animals, the lake. . .

Jessie was out there somewhere, all alone in the dark. And it was my fault! I had to find her before something terrible happened to her!

Dear Diary,

Help! I'm trapped in an art supply cupboard at Camp Evergreen and I can't get out!

Hold on a minute, Diary. I've got to go pound on the door again. Those little monsters who locked me in here are right outside – laughing their heads off!

Okay, I'm back. And still stuck here. I can't believe how I got into this mess!

It all started when I told my friends how much I wanted to come back to Camp Evergreen next year – because I've been having such an awesome summer.

"You'll be too old to come back," my friend Claire said.

"She's not too old to be a Junior Counsellor," my friend Allison pointed out.

Really? I thought. Cool! And the very next day, one

of the Junior Counsellors got sick and had to go home. So I volunteered to take his place – helping out with a cabin full of seven-year-old boys!

Big mistake. Those boys are a handful! And do they want to listen to anything a "stupid girl" has to say? No way.

Anyway, don't worry about me – yet. I think the air in the cupboard will last me at least a week. (Just kidding.) But the real question is: how am I going to win over those little boys when I get out of here?

Dear Diary,

"It's got to be here somewhere," I muttered. I dug around in my camp trunk, looking for the photograph of Andrew and me.

It's my favourite picture of him – the one we took when we first got together this summer. So there's no way I would have lost it, right?

But for some reason, it was missing.

I took every single T-shirt out of my trunk and piled all the stuff on my bed. The picture wasn't there. Then I sorted through the stack of mail from home. *Maybe it got mixed up with my letters*, I thought.

But no.

My heart started pounding a little. Because I knew

there was only one person who could have taken it.

Brooke.

The new girl who had just arrived at camp yesterday. The girl who had been friends with Andrew for five years.

The one who hated me.

Brooke must have taken it, I realised. That was the only logical answer. But how was I ever going to prove it?

mary-kateandashley

TWO of a kind ™

HarperCollins*Entertainment*

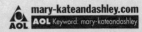

mary-kateandashley

TWO of a kind ™

mary-kateandashley

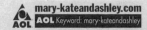

mary-kateandashley

Sweet 16

(1) Never Been Kissed	(0 00 714879 8)
(2) Wishes and Dreams	(0 00 714880 1)
(3) The Perfect Summer	(0 00 714881 X)

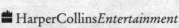

Mary-Kate and Ashley's latest exciting movie adventure

Available to own on video and **DVD** VIDEO 29th July 2002

Mary-Kate and Ashley in their latest movie adventure

Available on video from 11th March

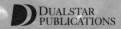

the **mary-kateandashley** brand

Fab freebie!

You can have loads of fun with this ultra-cool Glistening Stix from the **mary-kateandashley** brand.
Great glam looks for eyes, lips – or anywhere else you fancy!

All you have to do is **collect four tokens from four different books from the mary-kateandashley** brand
(no photocopies, please!), send them to us with your address
on the coupon below – and a groovy Glistening Stix will be on its way to you!

Go on, get collecting and sparkle like a star!

Real Books for Real Girls

It's What YOU Read

TOKEN

Name: ....

Address: ....

....

e-mail: ....

☐ Tick here if you do not wish to receive further information about children's books.

Send coupon to: **mary-kateandashley Marketing**,
HarperCollins Publishers, 77-85 Fulham Palace Road, Hammersmith, London W6 8JB.

Terms and conditions: proof of sending cannot be considered proof of receipt. Not redeemable for cash. 28 days delivery. Offer open to UK residents only. **Photocopies not accepted.**